DEVIANT

CHRONICLES OF PRIDE

Deviant- Chronicles of Pride
Edited & Compiled by Samhitha Reddy
Print Edition

First Published in India in 2021
Inkfeathers Publishing
New Delhi 110095

Copyright © Inkfeathers Publishing, 2021
Cover Design © 2021 Inkfeathers Publishing

ISBN 978-93-90882-12-0

www.inkfeathers.com

DEVIANT

CHRONICLES OF PRIDE

Edited & Compiled by

Samhitha Reddy

Inkfeathers Publishing

DISCLAIMER

The anthology "Deviant- Chronicles of Pride" is a collection of 9 stories and 27 poems by 22 authors who belong to different parts of the globe.

The anthology editor and the publisher have ensured to make the content as reader-friendly and plagiarism-free as possible. Unless otherwise indicated, all the names, characters, objects, businesses, places, events, incidents- whether physical/non-physical, real/unreal, tangible/ intangible in whatsoever description used in this book are either the product of the author's imagination or used in a fictitious manner. Any resemblance to actual persons, objects, entities, living or dead, or actual events is purely coincidental.

The stories and poems published in this book are solely owned by their respective authors and are no way intended to hurt anyone's religious, political, spiritual, brand, personal or fanatic beliefs and/or faith, whatsoever.

In case, any sort of plagiarism is detected in the stories and/or poems within this anthology or in case of any complaints or grievances or objections, neither the anthology editor, nor the publisher are to be held responsible.

CO-AUTHORED BY

Deborah Mejía, Amy Sutton, Niamh Donnelly,

D. L. Cordero, Penelope Epple, Celeste Skywalk

Niamh Hennessy, Vernajh Pinder, Aamir Hassan

Lily Rosengard, Catherine Guy, Taisha Guy, Adam Gaffen

Paul Williams, Ankur Mondal, Melanie Williams

Mollie Sambrook, Christy Pineau, Ashley Amber

Shelby Catalano, Tejaswi Subramanian, Abhiti Gupta

CONTENTS

Gay Pride

Bi Visibility

Trans Narratives

Queer Factor

Asexual Confessional

x

MEET THE EDITOR

Samhitha Reddy

Samhitha Reddy is a law graduate who is currently pursuing her MSc. in Human Rights at the London School of Economics and Political Science, London. As an aspiring lawyer, she wishes to pursue a career in international human rights and has been widely published in various leading law journals of India. A wanderer at heart, she is also an avid traveller and foodie. She has a growing passion for Indian mythology and history and is trying her hand at writing fiction. As a part of her first editorial venture, she has curated a two-volume anthology titled, "Shades of a Woman:

Navigating Society as a Woman", and "Liberation: Breaking the Glass Ceiling of Society'", where the writers share their experiences and inspiring stories about the women in their lives (or themselves) and their navigation through social structures and barriers. "Deviant: Chronicles of Pride" that is aimed at raising awareness about and acceptance of the LGBTQIA+ community, is her third editorial venture. A bookworm ever since she was young, it is hard to find her without a book in her hands and she's now chasing her dream of being a published author in addition to pursuing her passion in human rights.

EDITOR'S NOTE

"Who am I?" is a question we all ask ourselves at some point in our lives. When we are born into heteronormative societies with a preconceived notion of 'normal', one begins to feel ostracized and 'different' from a very young age. Thus, the arduous journey of self-discovery begins, oftentimes, alone and without a guiding light. This journey, many a time, is hidden and is often associated with feeling out of place, different, confused, and unaware of what labels to subscribe to, if at all we want to and at the extreme, shame and self-hate. Why? Because someone else has already decided our 'normal' for us. Unfortunately, not adhering to such implicit social rules can not only put us in the spotlight of verbal or even physical harassment but it can also be legally punished. Let's not forget that several countries around the world still sentence those in this community, namely those who show queer, homosexual or transgender tendencies and behaviours.

Heteronormativity is the privilege(ing) of heterosexuality that results in social pressures to fulfil and conform to binary gender roles, and it leads individuals to conceive themselves and their social worlds in particular ways. From the smallest character traits, like the way one walks or talks to the larger societal expectations of marriage, people are scrutinised and judged. What is expected of each individual is not always who they truly are or what they want for themselves. Dismissing 'different' character traits as quirks or brushing off homosexuality, bisexuality and transsexuality as a 'phase' coupled with the pressure of dressing/acting 'normally' and being in heterosexual relationships only serve as ways in which the oppression permeates society. Not only must one adhere to society's norms, but we are also forced to do so through the most important stage in life for the development of whom we will become: puberty. The inability to live a life in which one can reconcile the body with the mind results in one feeling 'othered' in their daily lives.

Hence, the unconscious and automatic assumptions of heteronormativity dictates the invalidation of all other types of sexual experiences, preferences, and identities, presenting them as abnormal to the masses. This thought process is everywhere around us and the LGBTQIA+ community has walked a long winding road with multiple obstacles to get to an era where the rest of the world has just barely started warming up and considering accepting the most palatable aspects of the community. It has not been easy, and it still is not. The stigma and judgement that emanates from the majorities often make it difficult to come to terms with who we are and create a positive self-perception of our identities and orientations. While this era may seem new to some of us, there are many LGBTQIA+ positive communities throughout history, which we are not taught about or are aware of, wherein trans-, intersex and queerness have been present and even celebrated.

Too often, the stories and voices of members of the LGBTQIA+ community go unheard. This compilation is my way of honouring the wondrous human beings who have shared their most vulnerable experiences with me and all the other people of the community out there who continue to battle unthinkable prejudice and inequity and do so with grace and immense courage.

This book is also my way of showing solidarity for this cause, hoping all those who read this collection of poetry and prose know that they are not alone on this journey. I pray that this book fosters visibility and leads the much-needed dialogues and conversations about sexual orientation, gender identity, mental health, diversity, and inclusivity. This book is the coming together of people from the community and a few allies, united by the common pursuit of spreading awareness and expressing oneself. The best way to celebrate the love and acceptance and acknowledge the struggle and the progress of the people of this vibrant community is to hear from them directly.

Storytelling is a highly effective tool (and my personal favourite) to raise awareness and foster acceptance, as is evident through the moving pieces enclosed in this book. Through the soulful work contained herein, the authors have moved to reclaim what is theirs and step into the light. Fighting shame and social stigma and marching on in the face of threats and violence – this book is not only an inspiring celebration of differences but also a declaration of self-acceptance and visibility. This project means a lot of things to a lot of people. For some, it is a period of reflection and introspection, for others, it is a celebration of how far the community has come, heartfelt gratitude to those who fought for the rights that were meant to be inherent to being human and for a few others, it is a realization that we still have some way to go.

Yet, the vast and varied life experiences narrated herein do not fully portray the diversity of the community. While I have tried to include diverse pieces from across the spectrum, it is impossible to ever capture the true complexity and finer nuances of the infinite experiences and identities of the community. However, the pieces in this book not only encompass the struggles of being a part of this marginalized community, the compounding nature of social inequality and oppression (intersectionality), but it also demonstrates the sense of liberation and accomplishment that one feels when owning up to and affirming their true selves.

Through this book, I strive to challenge the boundaries of (hetero)sexuality – to challenge some ways in which heterosexuality is created and maintained, to destabilize the ways in which gender hierarchies and social institutions and practices uphold heterosexuality above all else, and how sexuality and gender are misunderstood as only one layer in our complex and intersecting identities.

Until we achieve true equality in our minds and the outside world, this book will be relevant, and perhaps even after that, because the celebration of marginalised identities will always be vital to promote awareness and help encourage people to feel proud and comfortable in their own skin. We need to move from awareness and tolerance towards acceptance and celebration of the kaleidoscope of identities and colours the pride flag represents. For those who believe that legal recognition for this vibrant community is sufficient, I implore you to look deeper into your humanity and empathy, to open up and listen. Change is possible, we have seen it. We have to continue believing in a world in which we can all be our truest selves without fear.

Happy Reading,
Samhitha Reddy
Editor

Spectrum Stories

1
All Flowers Belong

Deborah Mejía

A Woman, A Peony
Sapphic Love
I do not really care for what you'd do to me
As long as you live free with the sun, with the sea
I think that what may hurt is you forgetting me
Once you drift, so fulfilled and independently,
While I just sit around and count the peonies,
Wishing to be brave and let myself unleashed,
To pray for cherry lips to tease eternally,
A lock made of our love, hearts beating ceaselessly

Secrets Kept
Asexual Romance
This love is quiet, subtle,
Known only to us both,
Like the discovery of flowers
Or a tea sparsely enjoyed,
But it is real, it is here

Transformation Illumination

Trans Pride

They tread the path
To loving themselves
More than ever,
To become their truths
Forever

Non-Conforming

Non-Binary and Agender Spectrum Pride

We rise above
The "either, or"
Being neither, being both
We are beyond words,
Feeling no envy,
Free like birds

Fluid

Genderfluid Pride

Feelings not set in stone
When there's much to behold
Unconstrained, unbound soul
I change like seasons, like water's flow
A force of nature, ready to venture

Spectrum

Asexual Spectrum

I catch the light through my lens

A first, after years of darkness

And I discover my reflection,

No longer a shadow not yet defined

I ascend into the rainbow

A being in the spectrum

The Lies We Tell to Survive

About the "Closeted" Life

With so much love,

Yet feeling so lonely,

I get by in my closet

With words of my own,

No hand to hold,

A world of paper,

A heart torn

And I Rise

Sapphic Love

I want you to think of me

When the moon wanes

When you catch my heart

From beneath the waves

Affections
Homosexual/Homoromantic
It is a connection
Unique to our own,
A kind of affection
That feels like home

Friends: Found Family
Aromantic Soulmates and Other Platonic Loves
Companions in life,
We read each other
Like well-loved books

Our paths engraved
By eternal ink
And shared dreams

Fairy Tale
Sapphic Love
The sweetest of whispers,
The caress of ink over paper,
The worlds that I create

That is where you and I meet

Made straight out of fiction,
Born from my heart,
You are the love of my life

Sunset, Comfort

Lesbian Love

I've found the place that you've blessed,
Where my dreams may lay to rest
Tucked in between the red plush pillows
Of your red lips, or hidden in your chest
A spot where I'm yearning,
A corner where I'm burning
Under your hair like willows

Look at me,
Remember the colour
Of the sunset
That made you and me

2

THE FEATHERED FOLK

Amy Sutton

Once there was a village, nestled in the crook of a blue, blue mountain range. Below them, rich marshlands stretched out, and above them, the sun would shine high in the day and the moon would sweep over the mountain range at night.

And this village had a secret. And like every good secret, everyone in the village knew about it. Sometimes – just sometimes – people in this village would start to sprout feathers.

Everybody knew about it but nobody talked about it, so although everybody knew about it nobody really understood it. No one knew exactly what it was, what caused it, what it did to you, what it meant. They knew it was different. Definitely strange. Not…bad necessarily. But it couldn't be good, because why would you have to keep something good a secret? And no one knew why only some people got it. Maybe it was like an illness. Which meant…maybe it was catching. Maybe it was dangerous. Maybe it was even…immoral somehow.

Nobody talked about it, but everybody knew about it because it had seeped into the stories and the nightmares of that village. Their ghost stories included terrifying monsters sprouting great feathered wings from their backs. A feather falling in a story was a sign of doom ahead. People with an affinity for birds were always the villains of the story. Everybody knew what to be afraid of. Everybody understood why the children of the village threw stones at the birds that flew into the village market. Everybody felt the edges of that secret in the quiet, angry, grieving stories of a parent talking about how they had 'lost' their child, even though no one had seen them sick or ill.

Everybody knew about it, but nobody talked about it, which meant there was nowhere to go, no elder to guide you, no one to talk to if you found it happening to you.

Makoto was not young enough to be called a child any more, but definitely not old enough to be regarded as an adult when they started to feel the prickling at their shoulder blades. Then, what they had thought was some rash on their shoulders turned into hard raised bumps, and peeking through the skin came the first tufts of down feathers. Makoto was terrified. To start with they covered themselves head to foot in thick cloth, even in the heat of summer, and refused to join their friends in stripping off and bathing in the river under the moonlight. They stopped speaking to their friends altogether, becoming more and more withdrawn, letting their hair hang loose and pulling their sleeves down further and further. But those feathers crept down Makoto's arms and up their neck until even the fullest covering would not hide them.

And so, Makoto went to the bathroom, locked the door, stripped down to nothing, and plucked every last feather from their skin. They plucked and plucked until not a feather was left, and they gathered up every scrap of down on the floor, stuffed them into a bag, hurried out of the house in the dead of night and burnt them out on the marshlands.

Every morning Makoto would wake up before everyone else and lock themselves in the bathroom, scouring every inch of their body, plucking any feather they could find growing, plucking until their skin was raw and bleeding. They would stuff those feathers into rubbish bags, burn them, bury them, flush them down the drains – whatever they could do to get rid of them.

No one knew Makoto's secret. They sat with their friends in the schoolyard and laughed with them as people told jokes where bird people were made the butt of violent jokes, and Makoto's soul wept because they felt so alone. What could their life be? Either their secret would be discovered and they would be cast out of the village, or they would have to live in hiding, tearing their feathers out for the rest of their life, and they didn't know which was worse.

Makoto's sorrow led to wandering out on the marshlands at night. And one night while they were wandering, and the moon was rising golden and full over those mountains, Makoto heard a beautiful, haunting sound. There was singing wending its way through the night air. Makoto looked up and saw shadows moving across the moon. A flock of birds was flying across the sky, singing this beautifully haunting song. And Makoto's heart was moved. Tears stood in their eyes. They watched as these beautiful, ethereal, graceful birds swept through the sky, circled, and landed in the marshy waters just before Makoto. It was a flock of crane birds, and as they approached, Makoto realised that there were words in the song - that the cranes were speaking and Makoto could understand.

The cranes sang a song of welcome as they approached. "Welcome child. Honour to you, child. We are glad to have found you."

And Makoto asked, "How can I understand you?"

The cranes replied, "Because you are one of us. For we are not normal cranes and you are not a normal human child. We are the Feathered Folk, and now we have found you, you can release your wings and fly free with us, and join us in our journeys across the world."

And Makoto fell to the floor and wept. Makoto lifted their thick kimono to show their scarred shoulders. "I have no wings, my siblings. I do not know how to fly. I cannot join you."

The cranes gathered around Makoto in a song of grieving and love. Their feathers pressed into Makoto's aching skin and it was soothed.

"Don't worry," the cranes said. "We will teach you."

And so, Makoto returned to their village. And every day they would search their body and pluck their feathers. But now they plucked gently, carefully, and stored each feather like a precious jewel in a pack hidden in the eaves of their house. Every night Makoto would hurry down the mountainside to the marsh waters and join the cranes, where they would show Makoto, the graceful movements needed to swoop and duck and fly, and the refrains of the haunting, beautiful crane song.

The moon rose and set and rose and set. The rainy season passed and the dry season passed. And a year and a day from when Makoto had first met the Feathered Folk, things were finally ready.

Makoto came down to the water's edge, bringing with them the pack from the eaves, filled with a year's worth of plucked feathers. Makoto opened the lid and laid each feather out, shining in the light of the moon. And the cranes gathered around, singing their haunting song, and began to sew those feathers into a cloak. Makoto sang and sewed with the cranes until the final feather was stitched. And then Makoto stepped into the marsh waters and the cranes draped the cloak of feathers around Makoto's shoulders. And at that moment, Makoto transformed into a crane.

The Feathered Folk opened their wings and soared towards the shining moon, and Makoto opened their wings as they had practised so many times before in human form, and joined them. Off they flew into the sky, singing the beautifully haunting song of the cranes, off to a world of new stories and new adventures.

Identities Beyond Boundaries

3
Explosion of Truth

Niamh Donnelly

The day I came out,
And I'm sure it had nothing to do
With the liquor on my tongue,
I felt a weight lifted.

I had locked myself away inside myself
And letting those words out,
It felt like I was feeling the sun on my face for the first time.

4
Landscapes

D.L. Cordero

Cleaving iceberg

        mother has left.

                Sunken ship

        father is gone.

Mountain

        raise yourself.

                Hot air balloon

        drift alone.

Foreign lands

        live as outsider.

Foreign lands

live as outsider.

Live as outsider

in foreign lands.

Live as outsider

outside.

5
Unidos

D.L. Cordero

touch as I touch
feel as I feel
mouths wide with our anger and joy
We expand, contract, flow
spill over as fruit and flower
bloom in morning, wither by night
We rebirth from seeds planted
 in soil made rich
 by Our vision and strength

6
Legacy

D.L. Cordero

We will love
and love
and love
and love
In the face of violence
we love ourselves
In the face of destruction
we love those like us
When the lashings tear
we love our skin
When the wounds bleed
we love our blood
and we love
and love
and love
and love

all that we have been and

all that we will be

Because we are blessed

and none can make better

Because we are glorious

y nuestra victoria viene

We have seen past the horizon

and know our children dance

in the fulfilment of our dreams

so we will love

and love

and love

past our final breaths.

7

We Are What You find Inside Stars

Penelope Epple

You'd think we were splitting the atom again.
"You're destroying nature!" they spit at us.
"Mutilation!"
"Abomination!"

All I can see is the fire in your eyes as you smile.
It lights up your cheeks and
makes your whole body dance
when you relax into your wonderful queerness.

Oh, my friends,
maybe we are splitting the atom again
the way stars have for millennia.
Maybe we are destruction,
burning away the restrictions
on what bodies, on what people can be.

8
Is It A Crime to Love?

Celeste Skywalk

The dainty pages of history were fading away,
As the fonts that were written through the invisible ink,
Some spaces were filled with mortal buildings.
Fifty that felt like fifty thousand and more.
Some voices were similar to a whisper,
From the past to the present could you admit.
It was still not safe,
To capture yourself as you were eyed.
Is it a crime to love?
For each sob would be filled in the bottle,
To be thrown across seas,
For the disease of love would be caught by whoever is reached.
It was an island,
Where all the burnt romances,
Craved salvation,
You found yourself getting swept by the waters underneath,

The seas that motioned the clouds to sympathise with your aching fears.

For one day,

The island would be for peculiars.

But we would have a few to name.

For one day love would be no crime.

9

A Whisper And A Rippling

Niamh Hennessey

I want to tear down the walls
And start a new town
Full of all the people who've ever felt alone
And tell them that I'm sorry they've never had a home.
I want to call the churches
And tumble them down.

To paint a different picture of salvation to a balm

To see the rockets launching
Rousing crowds to better times
And faith and love are curing
What beat us far behind.

A small clock in an alcove
Counts seconds while we dance
Between reality and caring

A tribe that's never blessed.

Of saxophones and smoky rooms
Windows left ajar
The mystery in the moonlight of
Wounds that heal to scars.

10
Deluded

Celeste Skywalk

Yesterday they denied the colours,

Would they accept her ever again?

One knows that after the sun meets the drops,

There will be no pain.

For a minute the sky was covered,

Grey and dark,

Why couldn't they pay homage to the rainbow,

Which fills the intricate skylark.

Her aesthetic feed that they praise,

Has no light,

The little things they would want to know.

There are a lot of battles to fight!

Can she paint herself in colours,

That are not dark as they want her to be,

If there would be a way out of the prism,

She could finally see!

She could finally live with glee.

11

A WAR WITH MYSELF

Vernajh Pinder

One time my therapist asked me, "How would you describe yourself in terms of sexuality?" Naturally, I knew this was coming, so I casually replied, "Bi-sexual." Of course, I was thinking this would be the end of it. However, his next question though simple, I was completely taken aback. His question was, "Are you comfortable being bi-sexual?" In my head, I wondered why he would say this to me. I really wanted to say, "No. No, the hell I am not." But my pride told me that I had to say, "Yes." In that regard, he explained to me that sometimes we claim a title, but we do not feel entirely comfortable with it, or in my case to make everyone feel better, we feign an identity. Trying to appease everyone else but ourselves. Despite all my efforts to rid myself of this thought, my thoughts kept coming back. I wondered whether I was comfortable with myself. In part, I believed that, but deep down in my heart, I knew I was not. I have drifted through my life like a feather in the wind, searching desperately for a place to land. Always walking on eggshells, feeling like I had swallowed packs of razor blades and I was choking on my blood. Constantly at war with myself because

I am hiding who I am inside because the world hates the person I am. Afraid that my queerness will offend someone to the point where they think my life matters less than theirs. Or, for them to believe that somehow my sins are darker and deeper than that of their own. An attitude of cavalier disregard towards those that are suffering. Sometimes these emotions are so overwhelming that I find myself crying, even when it feels like it does not seem to help. I long for the beach, the only place my mind ever finds solitude, and to let the oceans carry me home. My obsession with the ocean might be due to a desire to bathe in the ocean and erase all my fears, wipe all this pain away. A wish to drown everything in this ocean and emerge as a new person unafraid. Only, it is never that easy, is it? Hence, I spiral deeper down in despair and stare at the bottom of an empty glass, waiting for my refill, waiting for my courage to be poured into my cup again. To be carefree again, to finally feel an ounce of happiness. Having something to hang on to here, even if only for a moment. Where I do not have to feel anything, to be anything. Just to live, breathe, survive, and thrive. I often wonder, why do they hate us so much? Is it because the God that they pray to tells them to? Or is it because they do not understand us? They have been conditioned to hate us, never to understand us because if they tried to, then they would see that we are not much different. The only difference is who we chose to love. I am starting to learn that the unknown makes people uncomfortable, makes them feel vulnerable. In other instances, maybe it stirs up something inside them that they have not been able to come to terms with yet. Either way, an open heart, and mind are needed to move forward in the uncertainty. I long to feel comfortable in my skin, where I do not have to hide within the labyrinth I have created for myself; an inhabitant of a universe of my conception. Sometimes the noise on earth is so loud that we try to escape it, only to end up in space: cold, broken, and alone. Gasping for air, for comfort, for companionship. Craving to belong, to feel loved. Wishing someone would hold us together as we are falling apart. Maybe, if I were not so afraid to be happy, I could be happy. Maybe, some of us are meant to live out loud, and others, like myself, are meant to stay hidden. Perhaps, happiness is not a gift that all of us get to open. However, what if I am all wrong? What if there is happiness out there for every one of us, but we just have to take the first step? I hope one day I will be able to know for sure but, until then, I will hold on and continue to fight this ongoing war within myself.

12

JOURNEY TO FREEDOM

Aamir Hassain

My vision was blurred as I began to open my eyes to another day. Emotions were void but this wasn't necessarily anything unusual or different, nor did I view it as strange as it wasn't unfamiliar to me to feel this way. Bursting out of myself was yawn after yawn as I would stretch my whole body and reflect on another restless night. I would think about my dreams and my nightmares trying to piece them together and find any little detail that could reveal my subconscious thoughts and feelings.

On this particular morning, I remembered one particular horror that entered my mind through the night. In my nightmare, I had awoken in my bed and was spinning around and around until a sudden stop! I removed the covers from my body and could feel the buckets of sweat coming off my head and flowing down my body. All I could see was fire around me. Fire everywhere. Fire but nothing was burning. It was as though the fire was a cartoon and I was in my bed floating over it. I was too scared to move from my bed and place my foot on the ground as I didn't quite understand what was real and what was a reality. Was this Hell? Was this

Judgement Day? Was this it? Have I been that devious and evil in my life that there was no place for me in Heaven?

To this day, I cannot remember the rest of that dream. Either that or I have suppressed any and every memory associated with it. That day I woke up and continued with my existence. I was unaware of the damage I was causing to my mind and I never knew how to protect my mind either.

I looked into the mirror and saw nothing. Was I a vampire? Was I some sort of monster? I couldn't compute what was going on. Why was there nothing there? I screamed into the mirror and it was like screaming into an abyss. Nothing. I saw nothing there. Ringing sounds reverberated in my eardrums, in my skull.

The next thing I saw were pieces of the mirror all over my room. Who did this? Was it I who had lost control? Why did I lose control? I wanted to roll in the shards of broken glass and feel my insides crawling out of me. I did not want to be in this body...in this mind. Nothing was right and I knew why but I couldn't quite bring myself to believe it.

My sexuality tormented me as though it was a physical being choking me to death at every chance it got. I was suffocating daily under the strain of my intersectionality and torn apart by the shackles of an outdated belief system. This was the breaking point for me. This was rock bottom.

I knew I needed to be honest with myself. To build my strength back up and to say goodbye to my inner saboteur that kept telling me that I couldn't live my truth. This inner saboteur needed to stay within the realms of the empty and narrow-minded faces in society. It needn't be in my mind or soul. That would be too dangerous.

I began my descent down the stairs of my home and out into the world. The bitter cold air pierced my skin, and I did not gain from it the relief I expected. This air wasn't quite right. This air was tainted. I knew at this moment I would have to find a place in which I could feel free. A feeling I have never, ever felt before. Imagine that: freedom. Such a simple pleasure and joy felt by so many and I hadn't had a moment in my life to truly feel it.

I ran and I ran. I knew I had to get away. Not only from the plagues I was surrounded with but from my former self, that wasn't me and that wasn't who I am. I kept running and it felt as though I was in a vortex, how much longer could I run for?

Darkness struck.

Where was I? I couldn't see anything. I couldn't hear anything. I had gone to a path unknown.

Breathe in; breathe out. Breathe in; breathe out. Breathe in; breathe out.

I knew deep within I had escaped, and this had to be the final challenge to face. Could I overcome the last bit of fear, the last bit of dread, the last bit of trepidation, to finally see what was on the other side? Heart palpitations. Sweat seeping through my skin drenching my clothes. Breathe in; breathe out. Pulsating thoughts. Shaking limbs. Breathe in; breathe out. Numbing pain. Raging headache. Breathe in; breathe out.

I was going to win this final battle. My determination had reached a peak I never knew existed. I would scream away those voices that told me I wasn't good enough, that I couldn't be me and that I couldn't be free. I would scream with all my might. I am good enough. I can be me. I will be free. Slowly but surely a sense of relief started coming over me and I could feel the weight of the Universe lifting away from my shattered body. I may have seemed broken to some, but I knew this was the beginning of my recovery. This was truly the start of me simply being me and doing so unapologetically.

***

The sun rays beamed through the window to wake me. My eyes began to open, and a sense of clarity wavered through the air. I could feel every single emotion and it was incredible. I felt joy. I felt tranquillity. I felt at peace. I stretched my limbs as far as they could go and savoured the magical dreams I had. My sleep was perfect, and I loved to remember every detail of my dreams.

I moved out of bed and looked into the mirror. I smiled. I was proud of what I saw in front of me. I was proud of who I saw in front of me. A proud person. A person living their truth. A person that has allowed themselves to be happy. My reflection smiled and winked at me. He knew of the difficult journey to get here. He knew of the hurt and pain caused to get here. He knew that being here in this moment was correct. He and I knew our story and that way it shall remain.

We were proud.

We were free.

Envision
Transition

13
Intersectionality They Say

Lily Rosengard

Intersectionality they say,

Whilst they confine you to being in the 'ethnic minority' group

Or the mentally unwell kids over there

Or the gay ones there

But what about the overlap of true intersectionality?

What about Black queer women?

What about non-binary folk with negative mental health?

What about white trans women?

What about disabled straight Asian men?

The list goes on and on because we are never ending and always overflowing

We can't box people off

Into neat little packages

Avoiding the reality

Not allowing people their authenticity

Wanting to be

The one that helps and supports
Whilst ironically doing the exact opposite

This is why we need intersectionality
The idea that different systems of oppression affect us and
combine together

I am not what you perceive as a 'woman' one day,
Queer the other,
And mixed-race on the weekends,
I can't separate who I am just to please you

I am me
and I am all of me
all of the time

If you try to categorise life just to make things 'neat'
I am truly sad for you
As you must come to realise the world is messy and
unordered
This is our creative and beautiful reality
And it is time that we recognise that

14

ENCOUNTER WITH MYSELF

Abhiti Gupta

I am a thirty-year-old woman who decided to slide out of her cocoon a few months ago. I've been an openly bisexual cis woman for the past two years, and life has dramatically changed since I came out to myself. Writing this little something is a way for me to let go, accept who I am and convince myself that it is okay to be gay. Imagining myself talking about my reality is tough especially when my mental health has seen a series of ups and downs. Heterosexuality which is assumed to be the "normal situation" has never been the case with me. A past childhood experience of experimenting with sexuality has left a lasting impact. At a time when I was unaware of binaries being the norm and imagining every sexual encounter to be the same, irrespective of the gender of the person I was involved with, was of defining importance to me. I realised that I need to let go and face the world without being a victim of it. I want to deal with the world as a survivor.

The sexual encounters that I experienced as a child who had not even hit puberty were mostly consensual, and the ones that I assumed to be consensual kept my soul trapped in a shell when it became difficult for me to accept my truth.

Imagine a person in her late 20s coming out as queer and polyamorous; it is still a hard truth for me to accept. What frightened me was the thought that I would impregnate somebody. Unfortunately, this was and still is, the level of sex education in our country. So, it is not surprising but difficult to reconcile in my tiny head. The feeling you get when you are made to believe that intimacy is wrong and the shame associated with the world finding out can be debilitating. I wonder. what if the world never got to know about it? Kids experiment and they are hardly left alone so what is the probability that the parents will not find out about these experiments? Frankly, I am okay with this silence, because not everyone wants to talk to their parents about their childhood experiments.

I am able to engage with the language of experimentation only from the past year since I started seeing my psychiatrist. Before that, it haunted me as if I had committed a violent/criminal act and this continued to make me feel extremely guilty for the major part of my life.

Unfortunately, such an incident prevented me from coming to terms with my sexuality. I was in constant fear of someone finding out about it, especially because the people I was engaged with were so close to my family. I cannot fit myself in the same shoes even as an adult when the world around me is so heterosexual and being involved as a child is not something that anyone wants to see or think about. I can write about this part of my life because it was traumatic, but I do not want to be viewed as a victim of it because I still feel that I have been a perpetrator throughout and the reminders of those incidents still haunt me.

It is astonishing how I was a funny and outgoing child living with fear inside throughout, had nightmares and was even diagnosed with a neurological complication that impacted the rest of my childhood. I am one of those adults who does not feel the nostalgia of childhood or the need to reminisce about that part of my life. It was a struggle to be a child who had brain wires tangled up and who did not have the vocabulary or requisite knowledge to come out as queer. All of this topped with mental health issues that I was not diagnosed with back then.

I guess one of the reasons for such experimentation was my understanding of how I deserve love, neither from the family nor from outsiders. It was impossible to trust anyone, and share what I was going through. The only support, or I would say adoration, I got was from some of the pets my parents decided to keep at home. They showered all their love on me and helped me remain alive with their constant and consistent companionship.

I attempted to take my life a few times and the only outlet I could think of to let out all the frustration was my body. . It can be viewed as a sad journey but I would like to think that it was a matter of survivorship. Though my parents have lived a lower-middle-class life, I have remained someone who knows how to get most of her needs fulfilled. With the financial support from my parents and my wit, I was able to build a fairly good career for myself.

I identify as a queer woman but unless you have a decent gaydar it is difficult to figure that out and this has been my privilege. I got the opportunity to complete my education and aspire for more. My caste never became a barrier to the choices I made because it came with inner authority. I still have weaknesses as an individual but enough liberty to put them aside. Strangely, this realisation occurs to me as I write this piece and it is empowering. I have been in the social sector throughout my career because deep down. I wanted to support people who lacked the resources of opportunity due to their gender/sexuality. I cannot be more grateful about it; but does it give me the power over someone? A big NO.

I would now like to jump on directly to my coming out which took me several months. I was in a bubble when I first fell in love with a woman (at least when I first got to know that *Fuck! I am in love with a woman*). It was a beautiful bubble. I already was in a relationship but it did not stop me from falling in love again. I admired her and adored her. I also wanted to come out of my existing relationship because firstly, I did not want to cheat and secondly, I wanted to continue experimenting, though this experimentation was valid in my head.

My heart was mildly crushed when she did not love me back, but I had come out to myself and that was the achievement resulting from that love. At the same time, I broke up with the man I was in a relationship with and fortunately, it did not hurt. Many may judge me but it felt liberating and I, for the first time, was at peace. From then on, I was under the impression that I had adapted to "not getting hurt irrespective of the situation" but it was a lie. I'd rather not delve into this aspect as that is not the point I am trying to make through this narrative.

I had always been a person who has challenged the normal and spoken out against the norm. It didn't matter what it would cost but I knew I had to stand by what was right and what should be, otherwise, accepted. Lately, I came to the realisation of being a feminist but the structure of patriarchy was so ingrained in my mind that I could not understand that it is not the men who are the problem (though I still consciously decided not to date men) but it is the masculinity that they live with. What I wondered was can the women, non-binary folks, transmen be masculine to affect me? I do not want to imbibe you with my experience but that has been my reality. It is men who benefit from patriarchy but it is also people with the masculine understanding who are benefited from it. I do not want to convey that being masculine is wrong but taking benefit from the patriarchy that comes from masculinity has been a turn off for me.

I've spent almost half of my life on earth, worked in different spaces, met a lot of people, learnt many things, and emerged as a new person at different points but I guess life will treat me well only when I start to value it and I am trying to learn this art but the journey always continues. Stories don't write themselves, do they?

Sapphic
Classics

15

For A Woman Not Yet Mine

Deborah Mejía

Come into my bed,

I want to show you the scar you have not read

Pillow your head upon my chest,

Let me treasure you in your rest

Come into the sheets

So I may comfort you through your sleep

And memorize that pair of lips,

Trace the curve of your hips

Let me etch myself on your being

And chase this wave of feelings

I may not know your face,

But you've become the grace

Of my loneliest days

So, pillow your heart inside my chest
Let me love you with all I own,
With all the softness of my soul

Asexual Lesbian Love

16
Budding Love

Deborah Mejía

The maiden feeds
On the sweetest of honeys
Hidden in the tight bud
Of her carmine flower
She parts the silk folds,
Cherishes the slick lips
As red as her own,
And suckles on the milk
Of life and youth
That quenches the thirst,
That quietens the soul
The maiden drinks
From the finest of bowls
Syrup running free
Down the creamiest legs
A woman like her has known

And the softness of the touch

Of her lily of gold

Drowns her with delight

As they grow old

Erotic Lesbian Love

17

Picture of Peace

Niamh Donnelly

A cottage in the middle of a field

Of wildflowers, on the edge of a forest.

Morning cups of tea, overlooking the flowers

Blowing about in the breeze.

A glass of wine at night, in front of the fire,

With a purring cat by your side.

Labelled jars of dried herbs, home-cooked meals and silent days.

No interruptions from the media, from people living busier lives or those who don't agree with your "lifestyle".

A small cottage to share with my partner, a pet and maybe a child or two.

All of us learning to live with nature and relish in the small emotions of every day.

That is my picture of peace.

18
I Dreamt of You, Sugar

Catherine and Tasha Guy

I dreamt of you last night

I didn't dream we woke up together

I may have woken up too soon

But I dreamt of you

I dreamt I drank from you

Not only after you drank from me

But also after you drank from me

I dreamt that my juices were the only thing quenching your thirst

I saw how my calves clung while my thighs wrapped you tight like the Christmas gift you are, or almost were

I felt how my teeth abused my bottom lip when your neck was too far

I dreamt that like origami, you folded me to your liking

And yet I saw myself uncontrollably purposefully willingly arched serving you all of me

Cumming only when you asked me to

Allowing my flesh to be servient

But I liked it

I have a control issue

The type where it's necessary to hear you say my name

But somehow, I dreamt of you last night and my thighs
blocked your airwaves while my toes embraced your locks

My eyes fluttered to match your tongue

All the fluster in me gone

You are all woman and I felt you in my groin

I dreamt of you last night

I didn't dream we woke up together

I may have woken up too soon

Cuz the shallow waters that remained were only
reminiscence of the ocean we were floating in

The one we created, where the salt is all sugar

I hope you know that I can't swim

So unscrew gently.

Tell me it's not too late to taste you

Sugar

Ready to dig into your jar

I won't be wasteful

Ima take slow dips

Sips

Trips into a mind flip

Sugar

Can I

Sugar I need to taste you

Your refined grains
Your sand-like texture
Your fire to my flame
Your sweet sweet nectar
The sweet sweet pain
Sugar
Tell me it's not too late
Sugar
I want to be inside of you
I want to create
I want to use all the parts of you
Sugar
Sugar I want to be
What she could not be
For you
Sugar
I want you on my tongue
I want you on my fingertip
I want you on my nostrils
Sugar I want you to take me off my feet
Bring my body to its face
I want you to raise my heartbeat
Sugar
Tell me it's not too late to taste you
Sugar
I promise

As the sun rises and sets
As the moon controls the tide
As we spin on this earth closer and closer to our deaths
Sugar
Sugar
Tell me it's not too late to taste you
I promise I won't waste you

19
Queens and Queens

Celeste Skywalk

She wasn't a wallflower deluded,
What she was to a blossoming spring.
When the warning bells would ring,
She would submerge.
Underneath the deep blues,
She would talk to the mermaids.
She would whisper meekly of what is said,
What is done.
How can she be a prince,
Should have been one.
If that would make her royal princess realise,
What is said is what is done.
Would people pass glances,
As two Queens walk towards the throne.
Would they shower the petals,
Or with thorns would they be adorned.
But the rainbow is beautiful,

She loves how nature accepts,

While the sun can learn to reflect,

Why does the world deflect?

20
Love Is Only For The brave

Celeste Skywalk

We were all waiting to turn into dust,

For our souls could reunite.

If we could have spoken out.

If we could have seen the light.

Take me to the shrines,

And wash my sins away.

Do you know the meaning of happiness,

Is being gay!

Could have loved the one I wanted to,

Should have been open.

In the world which succumbs,

Could have been a voice.

For it wasn't the youngblood.

It wasn't an ambiguity,

She knew what it was,

Would have been accepted by the deity.

But not you,

As you appear to be supportive,
But stay numb as if the words,
Would reach dead ears,
Love was for the brave,
Could have been one!
Should have been one.

21

PARDON ME, DO YOU DO WEDDINGS?

Adam Gaffen

'We've got to talk.'

'And drink. It is vitally important that we talk, and drink. Now.'

Cass's face showed her confusion, so Kendra said, 'Kidding. What do you want to talk about?'

They were walking west along East Flamingo Road, gradually making their way into the tourists' part of town. The homes and buildings around them were small and crowded, but well-kept. There weren't many people about, being near dinner, and the sun was still bright in the summer sky.

Cass still cast nervous looks around before speaking again. 'How do you know all this?'

'It's amazing what you pick up,' began Kendra.

'Cut the crap! There is no way – none! - that a sensie actress and producer would know how to kill a man like that, or what to do with a commpad, or any of the other things that have kept us alive this afternoon!' She stopped and took

Kendra's arms, turning her to face her mesmerizing blue eyes. 'Tell me the truth, Kendra. If you love me, you'll tell me.'

'I'll tell you,' said Kendra. She started walking again, and Cass let her. They walked in silence for a couple blocks while Kendra composed her thoughts. Finally, she spoke again.

'I work for a company you've probably never heard of. We don't make anything; we don't advertise; hell, hardly anyone knows we exist! Our directors look for people who have the potential to make massive changes to the course of human history, and do whatever it takes to expedite their progress. Protection is one of our jobs. We also help with funding, provide research assistants, that sort of thing. In return, we get a tiny slice of the profits. About one percent, is what I was told. I've worked for them for six years now, from just before you went to work at HLC's optics division.'

'Uh-huh. And what's your job?' Cass's voice was cool, unemotional.

'Not research!' laughed Kendra, trying for levity and failing. 'I never did very well in science! You remember Bio? When we had to dissect the pig?'

A small, wistful smile tugged at Cass's lips. 'You fainted when I removed the skin.'

'That's about when I figured that I wouldn't be following you in your classes, and changed my focus.'

'Is that so? I always thought it was Billy Donovan in Econ.'

'Him too, though if I'd paid more attention to class, and less to him, maybe…'

After a moment of silence, Cass prompted her with, 'Maybe, what?'

'Maybe my business wouldn't have failed.'

'But – what? I thought – I saw your films!'

'I made plenty of money,' Kendra agreed. 'For other people. I got paid, but not real well, not at first. I was a dumb eighteen-year-old who'd never been away from home. I could whine and say they took advantage of me, but I knew what I was doing, what I wanted. I wanted sex, I wanted to get paid, and I didn't want to go to jail. Sensies. Simple.'

'Your production company – you're rich!'

'No, my production company failed. I was still performing as much as I could, to bring in more money, because I was losing it on the films I made.'

'What happened?'

Ken shrugged. 'Near as I can figure out, I just didn't watch the bottom line closely enough. I paid the actors too much, got paid too little on the distribution end, and took too much out as my cut. Stupid mistakes, but after a couple years I couldn't keep up anymore. That was in '06. One morning, I get email from this group, called themselves OutLook. They said they wanted to invest in my company, they loved my work and knew that they'd make a ton of money in the end.'

'So what was the catch?'

'There wasn't one – at first. Then they gave me a 'production manager', stone bitch named Amanda Talbott, and I gotta admit, she really knew her stuff! Amanda – no way you ever called her Mandy! - renegotiated all the contracts, got the books in order, generally straightened everything out. That went on a few months before the other shoe dropped. It was pretty gentle, actually. No threats, no violence.'

'How'd it happen?'

'Amanda and I were having our usual weekly meeting, and she just said, 'It's time for us to talk.' I said, 'Isn't that what we're doing?' and she just laughed at me. 'I mean about paying back OutLook.' 'Paying back?' 'You didn't think that it was a gift, did you?' It got loud from there, for a while. But once I calmed down, and gave her a chance, she explained it all pretty well. They offered to keep the company going, let me draw my salary, and all I had to do, at first, was go for training.'

'The training was done by the CIA – the Corporation for Intelligence and Assassination. I never knew where they took me; I was bound and blindfolded the whole trip'

'Wait a sec – back up. Assassination?'

'You asked, remember? Turned out, I have quite a talent for it.'

Cass nervously asked, 'Have you - '

'Killed? Yes. This was my eighteenth in self-defense.'

'Eighteen?' Cass looked at her friend and would-be bride warily.

'Plus twelve more on assignment,' Ken admitted. 'But they were all bad,' she assured Cass.

'And what was I? Another assignment?' Cass pulled her hand away.

'No! You weren't ever – *ever* – an assignment!' She grabbed Cass's hand back. 'When we met again at the premiere, that was the best thing that had happened to me in years! Everything after – falling in love, moving in together – none of that was planned or faked! That was real!'

'I want to believe you, Ken-doll, I really do.' Aiyana's voice cracked.

'Then believe this.' She dropped to her knees, heedless of the rough concrete, and gazed upward. 'Aiyana Rosewind Cassidy, I love you. Will you marry me? Tonight? Now?'

Aiyana fell as well, her arms wrapping around Kendra. 'I thought you said we couldn't? Not with our real names? And the fakes won't -'

'Fuck the fakes! I want you to be my wife tonight! It's a risk, using our real ID, but if I can't have you, now, legally, then running ain't worth it!'

No more words were necessary or, at that moment, possible.

***

'Do you, Kendra Marissa Foster-Briggs, take Aiyana to be your lawfully wedded wife, to have and to hold, for better or for worse, in sickness and in health, for richer or for poorer, being her rock and her joy, until death do you part?'

The minister – well, not really a minister. More of a professional wedding officiator, if you'd prefer – looked down at the two women.

They'd caught a taxi with a genuine human driver, who was more than pleased to take cash money for his services, to take them first to a bridal shop, then a jeweler's, followed by City Hall, and finally to the Chapel of the Resurrected Sirians (An Alienist Congregation, the sign below read). The wedding dresses were simple, compared to the ones they had worn only a few hours earlier. They were mirror images, both in white, keeping with Kendra's Amazonian style, though Aiyana was exposed on the right, while Kendra was exposed on the left. Both showed a plentiful length of leg, too.

The jeweler was eager to sell them wedding bands, though she insisted that, both being women, plain gold bands weren't enough. 'You need something sparkly,' she said, guiding them to their selection. 'I know the perfect ones.' She was right.

The rings she selected were identical in form – a bold, brilliant diamond in the center, flanked by a pair of smaller, identical jewels, one on either side. But the one she chose for Kendra to wear had topaz; Aiyana's, emerald. 'Obviously, the topaz, the emerald are your partner's eyes, so you know you are always in their thoughts. The diamond is for the purity and eternal nature of your love.' It was a line, obviously, but it wasn't necessary. They were sold and sized quickly.

They got a marriage license at the twenty-four-hour window in City Hall without any difficulty. Bribing the clerk to delay filing for a full day was simplicity as well; a five-hundred tucked under the completed form and a few whispered words and the problem was solved.

Nor was there any problem at the Chapel. 'We never drop weekend paperwork off before Monday no how,' said Reverend Hos Gaw Yu. But he pocketed his tip just as quickly as the county clerk.

Now they were here.

'I do,' whispered Kendra. She'd agreed to be asked first.

'And do you, Aiyana Rosewind Cassidy, take Kendra to be your lawfully wedded wife, to have and to hold, for better or for worse, in sickness and in health, for richer or for poorer, being her rock and her joy, until death do you part?'

'I do.'

'Then by the power granted me by the Church of the Resurrected Sirians and the Free City of Las Vegas, I pronounce you wife and wife! You may kiss your bride,' he finished.

A scattering of applause rose from the waiting celebrants, doubling as witnesses to the ceremony, as they each lifted a filmy veil from the other's face.

'You meant it,' said Aiyana, weeping.

'Of course, I did, you silly slitch! Now kiss me and take me home; I want you in my bed and I want you there now!'

The next few minutes were a blur of congratulations, signatures, and departures. Soon enough they were back with their tame taxi driver, who steered them toward the Luxor at their direction.

'We have about sixteen hours before we meet Dick,' said Kendra between kisses. 'What can we do with all that time?'

'We'll think of something.'

***

An excerpt from <u>*The Cassidy Chronicles, Volume One*</u>

It's 2113. On what was supposed to be their wedding day, Aiyana and Kendra were shocked to have the officiant attempt to kill Cass. Kendra took charge of their escape, revealing some previously-hidden skills. Now that they've fled their home in Los Alamos, in the Sonoran Republic, and ended up in Las Vegas Free State, it's time for a talk. What has Kendra been hiding? And can this relationship move forward?

About the series:

The Cassidy Chronicles is the first book in the Cassidy Chronicles series. The sequel, The Road to the Stars, picks up five years later. They're both working towards their dreams – Cass perfecting her invention, Kendra egging on the development of the world's first starship – and raising their daughters when they're approached by desperate politicians from within the successor to the United Nations. They believe that Cass & Ken's skills and resources can avert a global catastrophe, and so they're pulled into an interplanetary conflict they didn't even know existed. This time, the stakes are higher, the challenges are greater, and the surprises just keep coming! Volume Three, The Measure of Humanity, picks up a few months after the end of Volume Two. The conflict has cooled as both sides reassess and rebuild, but the opposition hasn't forgotten about Kendra. They'll go to any length to destroy what she's been building. Will they succeed? Or will they, once again, outwit and outsmart the opposition? The fourth book in the series is A Quiet Revolution and is/was released in April of 2021.

All books are available through Kindle Unlimited; or you can get them in paperback if you prefer holding your books!

Gay Pride

22

I CAN SEE YOU

Paul Williams

I never noticed how dark his eyes were. Had they always been like that? The pupil seemed to bleed out into the iris like a vortex of shadow, sucking in the deep umber pools. The air around us changed the moment I saw him. Something was wrong, and I couldn't place it for several minutes until I glanced around.

We sat together on a park bench. It was a sunny day, the kind that invited everyone from their homes to embrace the warmth. Dogs tread on the crisply mown grass, a spiced earthy scent clung to children dashing across the fields, staining their crisp jeans.

Noah tilted his head.

"Is something wrong?"

He sounded odd. Or maybe this curious energy clung to us now, for whatever reason.

"I-I don't know. I feel like something's missing, but…"

His face softened, and he slung an arm behind me, flicking his hand over my right shoulder. The comfort felt especially alien.

Taking a few deep breaths, I let the noise melt away. *Name things you can see.* I remembered.

Glossy playsets.

Cars lining the lot up a hill.

Dogs tripping over themselves to catch flying tennis balls.

People.

Had I been expecting someone to be here? Someone is missing...

"Hey, remember, deep breaths. Are you having anxiety again?"

I shook my head. No, no I couldn't be. This wasn't like before, something in the world was just *misplaced.*

I turned to look back at him and in his eyes, there was a glint of light, and it snapped in my brain.

The gray lady was gone.

I turned rapidly to see if she was somehow just out of sight, but there was only a soccer field. My eyes flossed through the crowd for her thin figure, but I came up empty.

"Do you want to go? We can grab some food or something."

I hadn't meant to, but his voice made me jump. His eyes were so much like hers, weren't they? So dark...but I had only ever seen her from afar. Her wet, black gaze ever peering at me, though I never paid much mind. Because she was always there, since before I could remember. But now, she wasn't. And here was Noah in her stead.

"Why are you looking at me like that, Eric? Please tell me what's bothering you. I want to help. I care about you."

I flinched again at the biting words. I was so uncomfortable I looked around again for the gray lady, but it was futile.

"Is it just weird that we're official now? I know it's scary."

I nodded. That was different as well. A relationship. I was happy, and that feeling was as true and beaming as the rays of sun hitting my skin. Now, feeling his hand gripping my shoulder as he scooted closer, we kissed. Perhaps this was my new normal.

23

I'M OTHERWISE A STRAIGHT MAN

Ankur Mondal

A closet is perhaps the safest space; no wonder everyone is comfortable hiding there. I take pride in myself for being out and open. However, the journey of "finding myself" has been different from what it looks like now. My best friend's mother always knew my love for him and was apprehensive about it too. This is something I got to know over a random drinking session with him when he confessed that he overheard his mother and wife talking about it.

I was aware that his wife always knew. He was surely taken aback by these unexpressed feelings of mine as he was another cis alpha male. But the rest of the evening was spent exactly like the others; with a lot of gossip and unsolicited life plans.

I moved to two schools but never understood why everyone treated me the same; differently. Yes, I have always been a very quiet and calm kid; both at school and home. It is also because my mother did not allow me to step out much to play with the other kids as she feared that I'll get spoiled and learn the wrong etiquette.

The understanding of mockery came pretty slow to me. During my junior school, I was christened female or sixer (translates to *chakka* in Hindi which means transgender). I never paid much attention to it as I could not relate those words to myself but I knew that it was not right. I was not an effeminate guy but, yes, there was a certain softness to my approach which broke the stereotypical portrayal of a cis man of this patriarchal society. My only refuge was in Music, Dance and Fine Arts; and there, the teachers didn't look down upon me or judge me. So, I immersed myself in those activities whenever there was free time so that no one could talk to me much.

The first shock of my life hit me hard when I had to change my school in seventh grade due to the family's financial crunch. Though this school spoke my native language it was hard to understand them. The narrow-mindedness of the students was directly proportional to the teachers, and that was the only place where they matched. I, now migrating from an English speaking school, landed up at a place where using this language in your regular communication seemed to align.

I did not know how to fit myself in this block. And here again, I became a centre of discussion for a few days. With time, the conversation further narrowed down back to my sexuality. I was given more names and this time it hit me real bad as they were raw and sounded brutal. A lady, who happened to be our English teacher, always had my back.

Once, during class, she overheard someone calling me 'ladies'. She simply asked the boy to stand up and give a valid reason for calling me by that name, to which he said, "Ma'am, he is always found hanging around girls and he doesn't even play any games. So all the boys in school call him by this name. I'm not the only one." She simply smiled and said firmly, "He knows how to greet and talk to a lady and hence the girls are comfortable talking to him, which you guys fail to do.

She asked him to take his seat and advised the class not to ever call me by that name but deep down I knew it was not the end. A few weeks later, it was early morning before the school assembly, I was asked by a few bullies from my class to follow them to the boy's washroom. I was scared but had no other option but to follow them. I was taken to one of the stalls and was asked to remove my pants. They wanted to ensure and confirm to the other boys that I was man enough and had the necessary tools to call myself one.

That was possibly the first time I felt so humiliated in my life. This left a real impact on my memory. During the mid-year of my secondary board session, I almost wanted to give up on my life. I did not go to school for a couple of days and honestly did not even want to go further. I wrote a letter (yes, I did not grow up in the cellular generation) to my then best friend about my feelings and the reason for not coming to school. Somehow the letter reached my English teacher and was read aloud in front of the class.

Later that evening, my friend came home to deliver me an apology greeting signed by my whole class. As I think about it now, that apology didn't matter much to me but then I had no other option than to move on. Honestly, the approach and behaviour of the kids had certainly changed towards me but it wasn't erased from their minds. This will sound funny, they started giving me advice on how to Man-up.

Gradually I crossed the hurdle of school and reached college. In this journey so far, the best takeaway was the guy I met during the final year of High School, who I now call my best friend.

Growing up as an 80s kid came with its own set of challenges. The narrow societal vision of gender norms did not even spare me during college. I was called more unique names like *Gur, Chawal* and whatnot. I was just learning more slang for my mockery. To be honest, I became more resilient towards that attitude. Slowly, I was also learning the art of neglecting what is not necessary.

As I was in an evening college, I started working during the day and after the lectures, I used to spend time with my mains. With time, those bruises were layered by their love and care. I was still a straight man, taking part in discussing and admiring women. Yes, puberty hit us long back.

We graduated and started the next phase of our life. My best friend, parallel to my knowledge, was seeing someone. The day he confessed, even I had a self-confession. The possessiveness of that truly made me realize that I was in love with my best friend, a man. A man I had known for almost six years now. A man I had never before even thought of romantically. But, there I was, in love.

It took me one wrong relationship with a woman a few years after my graduation to understand that I incline towards both sexes. A touch of a man was not new to me. I was touched many times and was even comforted by a man's hand whom I used to call and respect as an uncle; during my adolescence. After the breakup, I made a fake profile on Facebook and started talking to men. From there, I got to know about Planet Romeo (former men-4-men), a dating app for gay men.

There I met someone who opened the Pandora box of my identity quest. Growing up in a non-technical world, exploring and understanding yourself was next to impossible. The fear of society and getting judged stopped me from asking questions. But virtually, I had all the liberty to be who I wanted to be. The more I grew, the more I learned and developed a sense of self-respect. And slowly, I accepted myself for who I truly am.

By now, I was out to my close-knit. It was this man, who came much later in my life, who gave me the courage to stand out straight, holding his hand; and shout out to the world loud and clear that "I am GAY". When my parents got to know about it (indeed another great story), they were dead against it.

My Mom cried for months and still tries to convince me to marry a girl, whenever possible. Even that guy got married to a woman under family pressure, but I thank him for everything that he left behind, especially making space for the man who deserves it.

Even though the country is free from an abomination of a brutal law, homophobia is still a norm. Loving is still taboo. And when I walk out on the road, for them I'm still a straight man. It is a slow process but it is we who have to make people understand so that the coming generations would be able to take pride in who they are – because closets are for clothes, not for you and me."

Bi Visibility

24
Dichotomy

Melanie Williams

I kept trying to negate one for the other.

Because I love him, because I am attracted to him I cannot
love her.

I cannot.

I cannot be the thing that everyone around me hates, the
people my mother and the community pray for in church.

These feelings, these thoughts, they must be passing desires,
because, I like him.

But then there's her…

The girl that light moves around.

Who makes my chest swim and the heat rise in my cheeks
from my pelvic floor.

And I catch myself wanting to see more of her, to catch
glimpses of her naked wrists or stomach when she stretches
or reaches for the top shelves.

I survey the back of her thighs, her buttocks and I tell myself
it's out of competition, comparison.

I get excited when I notice her blouse is slightly see-through,
then feel my eyes burn and feel ashamed.

I notice how her hair always smells like coconut and her skin
in the winter smells like frangipanis from her hand lotion.
I look at the fullness of her bottom lip and wonder how soft
it would feel grazing against mine.
I ask myself this, and then I hate myself, and I hate her,
because it is easier than loving her.

25
Man And Woman

Niamh Donnelly

I find most homophobes are straight males
And maybe that's because
They never had to love someone
Just like them.

Loving a straight man
Is like jumping into the deep end
But you don't know if you will sink or float,
Mostly I drown.

Loving a woman is
Sleeping in a wildflower meadow on a sunny afternoon.
It's the ability to be free from society's shackles.

26

ONCE IN A BLUE MOON

Mollie Sambrook

O nce upon a blue moon, Girl sees a chance to escape the ropes of expectation wrapped around her by a conservative hometown and runs without looking back. This was how she was taught to be good, who and how to love, what and how to dress, which way and how to always behave.

Girl had been caged in a life that was just good enough- never questioned what it was like in the wild. Girl had lost her voice at seven years old where she learnt how to fit into the space the world cut out for her. She pulled in her elbows, dropped her shoulders, held her breath. But all that condensing took its toll, started to make her ill. All of her quiet made room for so much more listening. Girl listens to society, listens to others, until when she tries to listen to herself, she's become an echo. Her voice comes back indoctrinated, full of spite and rules and hatred. Now Girl doesn't know how to let go, Girl has to keep herself under wraps, Girl shakes with the effort, with the terror of what will happen if she stops being what she is supposed to be.

Girl at eighteen finds adversity. Full of a new universe- she watches the stars and their alignment, holds the hands of an energetic Pisces who shows her how to let go, a Libra full of so much love that she sometimes cuts herself open to let it all out. They watch the Girl, glances full of studying, full of figuring out. Girl opens up, tumbles out of herself, still won't take her hands off her deepest secret.

Girl thinks they have been waiting for her to say it for years now. Girl thinks they're all holding their breath too. Girl has only just come to terms with it herself, doesn't think it makes it any easier to say it out loud. Her voice has always been muted, speaking in sentences cut short, words are chosen so specifically that she's able to articulate over the background noise. So, when Girl can't keep her mouth shut, when she can't stop talking, only those closest to her know to make sure to listen, especially to what she isn't saying.

Sometimes Girl drops into static.

Girl doesn't just have a nervous system; she is a nervous system. Girl wants to know what it's like to not feel eyes on her, Girl wants to know what it's like to not care about who's watching. Girl feels like the world might have told her that she was a dog when really, she is a wolf. Girl wonders how she'd feel if she grew up without the judgement of society on her back.

Girl wants to be done with pretending; she wants something real. Girl doesn't understand, full of loyalty, why people can choose anything but listening to their hearts. Girl born with the disease of empathy would follow love anywhere blind and stumbling, down grass hills or concrete stairs or sand stretched horizons. Girl would follow love down hollows and let it grab her by her hair, dragging a broken spine over razor blades. Girl is tired, sick of people not having the drive to see things through, sick of people that won't go through the pain that comes before paradise, the hurt that has to happen for there to be comfort. Girl knows that in this- she is a hypocrite.

Girl and Pisces move into one room of the flat, push the beds together and spend all of a year learning how to tangle themselves together. Their clothes become one and Girl's self-worth skyrockets because Pisces shows her how to know what she wants, how to wear what she likes and move how she's been longing to. Pisces somehow blindfolds all the people Girl thought were watching. Girl wonders what it would be like to kiss Pisces and the ease that had settled inside her starts to disrupt again. Pisces gets bored with being the one to hold the both of them up and finds other projects to work on. Pisces gets swept up in ladders and climbing and what it means to be popular. Girl tries to keep up but doesn't think it should be so much of an effort to keep hold of her hand. Pisces laughs one night when they're three shots down, let's go of Girl's spirit-soaked fingers to point at a hairstyle cropped short, she says,

"Lesbian Linda."

Grief in her eyes, Girl spends the next two years learning which limbs belong to her, which ones to take back.

Girl wonders if she is one of a kind, Girl knows she might well be, purely because of the way that the very word girl has been shaped by girls. Girls and their bright eyes in bathroom stalls, with smiles and compliments reflected in the mirrors. Girls and their honey voices, "get home safe" their "I'll pretend to know you so you don't get hurt." Spikey girls and giggling girls and the "I'll hold your hand if you need it," - girls. Girl gets caught off guard when her eyes start to open when she starts to see the light. Girl feels herself grow through the ceiling; Girl feels like she's picking herself out of the rubble. It doesn't feel like so much of wreckage, more like she's bringing down an empire that society has built inside of her and something deep within her starts to breathe.

Girl's friendships feel like a safe haven, have always been built upon touch.

In drunken dreamscapes she dances with a friend who makes her laugh like a Leo, she feels at home, pulls her close and asks,

"Which field do you play for?"

Girl takes a breath, pretending she's not losing air quicker than she's gaining it,

"I don't know," her heart picks up and races faster than the beat that starts to vibrate all the air around her, "maybe both."

"You've never with a-"

Girl shakes her head, feels the colour rush to her already wine-rosy cheeks. Her friend draws back to meet her eyes and Girl doesn't feel like she deserves their understanding. Girl loses all touch as Leo puts inches between them. She takes Girl's fingers, gets rid of her frown by spinning her around as she studies.

"But you've wanted to?" The question is quiet, Girl knows Leo won't bring it up again and she's grateful for it but also wonders what it would be like to rip it off like a bandage.

"I don't have much bravery," Girl admits.

Leo throws a smile as her forehead drops down again to brush Girl's cheek and her breath is warm on Girl's neck and everything is safe but everything is burning.

"It's not brave to refuse to feel, it's cowardice. It'll be easier, to give up the fight."

Girl still doesn't know what to say, Girl has her hands around her own throat, Girl fears attention, fears being different. Girl is choked by her own morals and what it means to be free.

Girl, weeks later, bathed in the glow of the night, looks ethereal. A crystal hangs from a chain around her neck, glints in the light collects a wild energy. All of this may have been about the moon, not the sun, and Girl didn't even know it.

Her Libra, in retrograde, has her arms wrapped around her knees as the stars hang low. She points up, says,

"The second full moon this month."

Girl looks up under its silver light, rests her head on Libra's shoulder, wonders why it's always her and Libra there together when the world ends and starts again. Girl wonders why, like soulmates, they always bleed out together. She doesn't know what it is that causes all the spilling when she's around her but whatever it is it's always an opening.

Libra's hair is so pale in the glow it looks blue and she turns to Girl with a kind of safety blanket in her eyes, with open arms that say, I'll catch you. Girl would trade a thousand days for more like this, with her. A part of only two per cent of the population, the green in Libra's eyes plays with nature and Girl wonders if she'll ever find others as rare as her. She wonders if she'll spend the rest of her life searching. But Libra has always said she's not going anywhere.

Girl feels the honesty being pulled out of her like a tide. Girl knows that that's what the story is, what anyone's story is, their biggest truth. Girl knows if she's ever going to write the end, she's going to have to tell the world hers. Girl says,

"We don't get to choose who we fall in love with, do we? No matter how much we want to control it."

A few fireflies glow dimly in the grass, hover upwards so that when Libra turns to her there's a distracted awe on her face. She looks into the distance, attentive in the way she's pretending she's not- a soft grin, shakes her head no. She always knows when Girl needs a little less weight.

"The problem is you keep trying to use your eyes to see."

Girl is taken back to all the times Libra has told her before, "I've never met someone with a heart like yours, it's fucking massive," "you've got the biggest heart of us all," "your heart is so damn enormous."

If Girl's heart is open to everyone no matter who they are, regardless of gender, why is she holding it all in? Why can't she say it? Girl doesn't want to be who they told her she has to be anymore. Girl doesn't know why she's let herself be moved by puppeteers since she was a child. Girl doesn't know why she's been the puppet and the one to pull the strings simultaneously.

Libra leans into Girl's side, Girl wants to say, who am I to you?

Girl thinks Libra would say, it doesn't matter what anyone else thinks. You've always been you to me.

Girl knows everything Libra would say before she says it now.

Girl thinks she trusts Libra with her life, with everything that she has. Girl thinks if everyone continued to love her like that, with no expectations, no what-ifs, not despite but because of, then she might just be free.

She wonders what will happen if she says it, just this once.

"I have a truth for you. I don't think it's important to me," Girl says. And Libra's attention on her face feels like a desert's first rainfall.

"If I love boys then I think I'm in love with girls too."

And the world doesn't end, and the world starts.

Trans Narratives

27
I Am A Trans Woman And I Am Tired

Christy Pineau

I am a trans woman, and I am tired.
When I walk around the city streets,
I wonder how many of me have before and
felt the same looks of disgust follow their back like a shadow.

I imagine a future where I will have more
to harvest than the fact that the last X number of years has
ended.

The rest of the "alphabet soup" I'm lumped with
get their praise for doing things that were heroic,
while my people are jailed for being on the wrong street in
the wrong dress.

I went to an LGBT movie night at the library once.

Every night of the week they were playing some sort of movie

featuring an LGBT hero or pioneer;

Their lives were documented so fully and detailed,

they even knew the last time Harvey Milk drank Milk before he was assassinated!

Even though these were not my "kind",

I felt honour and pride for the community I was a part of.

I almost couldn't fall asleep the night before

they were to show the "T" hero,

I tried to guess who it was going to be,

and I couldn't think of anybody,

because the heroes of my people were never celebrated.

Marsha P. Johnson threw the first shot glass

at Stonewall and died of AIDS a few years later.

Another statistic, another reason why the dirty homos,

should have never been allowed in our bars and schools.

I felt all of these feelings of fear,

and confusion about just where I come from,

melt off my back as I walked into the library.

And for it to all come tumbling back,

when I saw they chose Boys Don't Cry.

The story of Brandon Teena.

The young trans man who was raped

and murdered by his friends

when he was discovered to be trans.

I re-read the poster on my way out of the library.

"Come witness the legacies of the pioneers of the LGBT
movement!"

I was wondering when our legacy,

would finally be revealed and

we would mark our name

somewhere other than on a gravestone.

Then I realized,

that even to those that are supposedly our own kind,

this IS my legacy.

Death. Loss.

Unaccepting family. Lost relationships.

Sex work. Addiction.

I am a trans woman and I feel so defeated.

The rest of pride month,

I walked the rainbow crosswalk

the government painted for "us" and
tried my best to see that as acceptance.

Even when we pave our own roads,
people run them over anyway.

Then they call it progress because
they never had to look back
at the carcasses
they left laying out on the street.

When the rain started a couple of months later,
the rainbow markings on the pavement had all but washed
off.

But knowing that they were there once before
is better than it never having been there at all, right?

June gave us some beautiful weather,
but for the last 4 days, it poured all day,
and drag queen bingo and
the queer speed dating socials were all cancelled,
much to everyone's disappointment.

I am a trans woman, and I bite my tongue.
I bite it because LGB pride month is a special event for
everybody.

As those drag queens would say,
the "tea" is that my supposed brothers and sisters
who are supposed to meet me
with compassion and solidarity,
all try to ignore that I am even there.

For any of you who read this,
anywhere out there, regardless of your identity,
take a close look at the group of friends you keep,
and try to look between the shadows
for what could possibly be
the remnants of someone like me,
who is no longer around,
either by death or
because those who brought us out into the light,
pushed us back in the dark
when they realized that we were dangerous.

I am a trans woman and I am tired.

It has been raining for 5 days now.

Yet for the past 3 years of this new existence,

I try to remember what the sun feels like.

Queer Factor

28
Our Queer Thoughts

The Queer Community & Lily Rosengard

my queer thoughts: part I

Queer means protest

Queer means being full of pride because you are proud

Queer means stop fucking judging others

Queer means being true to who you are

Queer means liberating yourself from societies conventions

Queer means unlearning

Queer means re-understanding

Queer means making no assumptions

Queer means looking beyond surface relations

Queer means pride is so so so much more than Pride™

Queer means never forget that pride started as a riot

Queer means pride was a movement was started by Black trans women

Queer means we need to stop white-rainbow washing history

Queer means we need more than just rainbow logos and sandwiches

Queer means no pride without liberation

Queer means fighting for trans rights

Queer means Black Lives Matter

Queer means Stop Asian Hate

Queer means End Islamophobia

Queer means End the Occupation

Queer means all of it and then some

Queer means never giving up for justice

Queer means swiping your dating profile from societies' default of 'men' to 'everyone'

Queer means subvert your 'nice normal of acceptability'

Queer means doing your best in a world that wants to categorise you

Queer means turning internalised shame into joy

Queer means making yourself visible even though it feels safer to stay invisible

Queer means beginning to be truthful to yourself so you can share your truth with others

Queer means a community of QTs

Queer means finding your community

Queer means coming out to your loved ones and them telling you you're not trans and you screaming back 'how can you be so ignorant, hurtful, stigmatising and unaccepting all at once'

Queer means coming out again because they didn't believe you the first time

Queer means not coming out again because you're tired of not being accepted or believed

Queer means your mental health is 'blamed' for your queerness

Queer means having to explain the definition of queer for the 100th time

Queer means definitions shift & are not the same as 50 years ago so stop telling me otherwise

Queer means stop invalidating my lived experiences

Queer means sometimes just not talking about it because I'm tired of explaining myself

Queer means not just surface level

Queer means not just a phase

Queer means it was never just a phase

Queer means I am worthy

Queer means I am my own person and I can decide how to define myself without the presuppositions & your assumptions of me

Queer means it's a journey... for others to understand you

Queer means not always being out for your own safety & mental health

Queer means always being out because of your mental health

Queer means people still don't believe you when you tell them you're queer even if they've read this far because they haven't met any of the women and non-binary folk you've dated but only the men

Queer means you wonder why people aren't out when society is rife with homophobia & your language is violent

my queer thoughts: part II

Queer means finding your supportive love bubbles and surrounding yourself with your queer siblings

Queer means I feel confident in disclosing this to you today but I might not tomorrow

Queer means openness

Queer means closedness

Queer means struggle

Queer means riot

Queer means rights

Queer means my rights don't mean you have lesser rights

(it's not pie)

Queer is power

Queer is powerless

Queer is power

Queer means meaningless sex

Queer means meaningful sex

Queer means sex, or no sex

(No, queer sex is not your 'sexy fetish')

Queer does not mean basically straight if you're read as 'woman' but basically gay if you're read as 'man'

Queer means fuck you

Queer means we might fuck –

or might not

Queer means meeting you and your friends at a busy student nightclub and making out against a pillar on the top floor whilst straight men ogle

(straight men FUCK OFF AND STOP OGLING)

Queer means moving the sofa outside to watch documentaries & eat strawberries

Queer means saving up your queerness for freedom in a new city

Queer means moving country to be you

Queer means moving back again, means feeling you've gone backwards

Queer means not growing up seeing people like you in the mainstream

Queer means not understanding if in that moment you fancy everyone or you fancy no one

Queer means coming out as bi and then pan and then queer and then realising labels are bullshit and meant to box us in so fuck it

Queer means what's it anyone else's business what I choose to do with my life

Queer means opening the door and a sausage dog escaping through the feet of the Hungarian Vizsla dog and us running after them with me in my slippers on our first date

Queer means picnics in the park and you taking great photos of me for the gram

Queer means responding to their dating profile pic with a queen emoji and saying you have the exact same top in blue

Queer means being simultaneously turned on yet jealous of their bum

Queer means being open

Queer means not being open

Queer means wholesome

Queer means not wholesome

Queer means laughing together at the paradox of knowing more about what to do with a body with a penis than with a body that resembles your own

Queer means tenderness

Queer means roughness

Queer means making it up as you go and trusting your instincts

Queer means other people making it their business what you choose to do with your life even though they wouldn't give a shit if it was a hetero-relationship

Queer means everyone's opinion and not your own

Queer means sniggers

Queer means belittled

Queer means you're simultaneously visible yet invisible

Queer means you're not a 'proper queer' because you've never brought home a woman

Queer means 'oh it's just a phase'

Queer means trust me, it's not a phase

Queer means fuck you

Queer means fuck me

Queer means what the fuck, what is going on

Queer means fuck - this is great

Queer means queen

Queer means yes I'm your queen

Queer means no you're my queen

Queer means WE'RE BOTH FUCKING QUEENS – THERES MORE THAN ENOUGH QUEENS TO GO AROUND

Queer means praying not to bump into anyone you know and making up a backstory about being colleagues in your mind

Queer means recognising that is heteronormative bullshit but realising you too are part of the system

Queer is hating yourself for having this conversation within your mind whilst sitting opposite such a wonderful, shining human

Queer is not knowing who is leaning in for the kiss so you both lean in and bump noses

Queer is going to the cinema on a date like a 12-year-old and crying like a baby at A Star is Born

Queer is reinventing dating conventions

Queer is them texting you after saying I think we're better just as friends and now two years on you still like each other's pictures and comment with the fire emoji

Queer means luv, lurve and love

Queer means it's a whole loada mess but I wouldn't change it for the world

our queer thoughts – from the community: part III*

Queer means am I queer enough?

Queer means you have always been queer enough.

Queer means who is the gatekeeper of queerness?

Queer means there is no gatekeeper of queerness!

Queer truly does mean you are queer enough –

you have always been not just queer 'enough' –

but queer abundant

Queer means community, history and freedom

Queer means out and proud, queer and loud, after fear and doubt in silence for so long

Queer means touching freedom with your fingertips and not drawing back, not running scared, but taking hold, feeling the static shock and knowing it's the start of a second life, fuller, brighter

Queer means refusing to fit in and embracing the differences

Queer means embracing the ever-changing parts of you

Queer means recognising that sexuality and gender are a spectrum that we exist at different stages throughout our lives

Queer means having the ability to express yourself honestly in the moment - not letting the pain of the past or expectations about the future define you in the present

Queer means the only definition that matters, is yours

Queer means relating to any love, no matter their gender (or none)

Queer means being open-minded, open-hearted and non-judgemental

Queer means educating ourselves about issues we might not know about within LGBTQIA+

Queer means LGBTQIA+ is not a monolith

Queer means your relationship status does not affect your sexuality

Queer means being in a hetero-relationship doesn't mean you're therefore straight

Queer means feeling constant imposter syndrome that you're taking up space and don't belong

Queer means never feeling imposter syndrome because this is your space and you do belong

Queer means there is a never-ending process of loving who I am and not letting society dictate how I evolve as a queer human

Queer means me, us, them
Queer means choosing your family
Queer means home.

* after releasing the first two sections of this poem, I decided to crowd source responses from the queer community to come up with a joint poem. It is thus a collective effort and so is hands down my ultimate favourite because it not only means and shows the power of community, but it IS community! It is OUR poem.

29
Yes Queer As In

Lily Rosengard

Queer as in I
As in no not straight and not bi
As no I'm not just referring to queer eye
As in I cannot keep living a lie
No matter how hard I try
To fall in love again with another guy
Because I need to put me
Myself first
I do not understand why
I continue to be judged by
Who I want to get to know
Who I date
Who I fancy
Who I look into the eyes of
And feel good and happy and fuzzy and warm and wanted.

30
Never Justify Your Queer

Lily Rosengard

Queer is me
Pride pride always pride
Queer as fuck
Destroy the binary

31
Queers Being Queer With Other Queers

Lily Rosengard

Queers eating vegan gluten-free curry at the bottom of the crag,

chatting, conscious partying, eating disorders, ballet.

Psych Ward, Alcoholics Anonymous, Rice.

Drugs, shame, cards.

Religion, Family, Tattoos.

polyamory, women, the morning after pill.

Oh, to be queer but not shamed for not being gay or not being straight.

For being in outward-facing heteronormative couples but with hearts unrestrained to the possibility of more light,

Of letting the joy of others in,

But still be in love.

I can learn so much from the queerness that surrounds me these days –

And I am happy.

I'm not too straight to join the club or too gay to join it too.
What a space of love and individuality

32

NEURO-QUEER: FINDING A COMMON LANGUAGE FOR MY HEART AND BRAIN

Tejaswi Subramanian

I remember my first love telling me, on a rainy night in Goa, that marriage was a practical institution that I was too weird for. They seemed to imply that my love was erratic and ricocheted off walls and people alike, piercing straight through the hearts of some and bouncing off within an inch of others, rarely returning to me due to its reckless energy. Its passion was turned outward, intensely taking in the sights and sounds of fruit sellers, madaris, snake-charmers, distant ravens, bellowing frogs, and the rain dancing on the surface of freshly-filled puddles, with mud slowly transforming into delicious sludge. My love ran amok, wild, uncontrollable, passionate, without any performance, headfirst wherever it felt received. I gave freely, with no inhibitions or limiting notion, I formed relationships with a sunflower headband that my best friend picked up before moving out of London, a light scarf that smelt of my grandmother, unsullied by the invasive scent of the fabric softener, a dog-eared invite that a former love shyly handed over to me hoping that I would notice the attempt to make plans for Valentine's Day, and a keychain that a school friend had bought for me so I would not lose my bicycle keys ever again at school. At that moment I felt incredibly seen and equally rejected.

I felt like a square peg trying to fit into a round hole, wondering if it made me less desirable to have around. I didn't know what I was doing wrong (which I now realize I wasn't at all), but I was not able to mask and contort myself into this object of desire that one would want to keep around. I had failed at reigning in my love and comporting in a manner that was convenient for the people I loved. My stitches burst open and bled in grief and relief. Somehow, they had set me free. They had gently nudged me out of the cramped cupboard that I was calling my home. I could now behave in all the ways that came naturally to me.

For the longest time, my identity evaded the vocabulary I was presented with; but it remained secure in the eye of my imagination, lush with metaphors and symbolism, strange purple-tentacled flowers blooming out of a mutated wasteland of broken hearts, slimy confetti strewn over the carefully-roasted seed of a human with more head than heart, no liver but all shot nerves. It made my love echo off 'improper' people, ('edge cases' as one friend affectionately put), the wrong gender, those who don't make enough money, whose parents do not drive impressive cars, whose walls are not tall enough to absorb the pained screeches from within, but whose hearts I could finally call home and forged a connection with that couldn't be severed by distance or time.

The madness of my whimsical heart was finally diagnosed as queer by Dr. Mary Jane and her aide, Tank Girl, as documented by the male gaze in Gorillaz, from which the story has to be reclaimed, for that's whose vocabulary I must retell my story in.

I want to be able to be understood the way *thathi* understood me on the days that I just lay by her side on weekends, exhausted and spent, but clutching onto her waist. I want to be able to be chosen the way *thatha* rarely told anybody that he loved them, except for me. I want to be left a legacy like that of my [other] *thatha's* notebooks where he had scribbled words, he had learnt from reading books, urging me to express myself by exploring language. I want to be reassured the way *thathi* did with her sympathetic silence. There are so many ways that I seek to be loved, and I walk around, with raw nerve endings that uninhibitedly spray sparks at the slightest hint of affection.

Those who seemed eager to yield to the aspiration of monogamy would often tell me that I had asked too much of them. To this, I would acquiesce, excusing myself from the equation, struggling to let go as it meant walking around carrying the grief of a lost connection – a rarity in my life where I was constantly treated like a smokescreen. People projected all sorts of ideas onto my blank slate, cementing my place in the blind spot on the Johari window. Gender expectations (foremost of which is emotional labour), social norms, for that fetishized *je ne sais quoi* to remain unmasked.

I couldn't come to terms with my queerness without admitting my neurodivergence. Both these parts of myself had sprung out of each other, like a pretzel or an ouroboros, like the soulmates described by Plato in *The Symposium*: unnervingly overwhelming for Zeus' comfort and ego, feeding off of each other's strengths when together and lost without purpose or meaning when separated and left to be longing.

It feels complete to introduce myself as neuroqueer, akin to telling someone that I am a colour wheel, instead of allowing people to perceive me as disparate colours that shone differently in different lights. Having a vocabulary that I resonated with allowed me to straddle between the Open and Blind quadrants of the Johari Window, express without shame or hesitance, and therefore build intimacy where I wanted, playfully (instead of with an uncharacteristic and aching vulnerability).

Some days, I feel bitter for not having the vocabulary to share my identity freely early on in my life. For not being able to explore in childhood, as much as I would have liked to. For struggling to engage in play, because of expectations to mask – by loved ones and public institutions alike. But slowly as I learnt the language of neurodivergence and queerness better, it was like I was slowly growing flesh & bones into a skin suit, taking space in ways that bloomed out of the eye of my imagination, lush with metaphors and symbolism, strange purple-tentacled flowers blooming out of a mutated wasteland of broken hearts, slimy confetti strewn over the carefully-roasted seed of a human with more head than heart, no liver but all shot nerves.

Asexual
Confessional

33
Ace of Hearts

Ashley Amber

Ace used to be a playing card. Spades, clubs, diamonds, hearts…

Hearts.

It's like some kind of joke. Ace of hearts.

As if anyone could find love when they were like this.

Ace used to be a grade. A+, excellent, gold star, 100 percent…

100 percent.

Nothing about it feels whole. It's like being the tiniest sliver on the pie chart.

As if anyone could feel 100 percent when they were like this.

Ace used to be slang. Cool, awesome, rockin', out of this world...

Out of this world.

Like an alien. That's what it feels like sometimes.

As if anyone could be from planet Earth when they were like this.

Now, ace is a name. A definition, a label, a peculiarity, a sexual orientation...

Sexual orientation.

This one has to be a joke.

As if anyone would feel sexual when they were like this.

Ace is a flag. Black, grey, white, purple...

Purple.

More than a colour, it celebrates a community. Because I'm not the only one.

As if anyone would be the only one when they were like this...

When they were asexual.

34
Almost Love

Niamh Hennessey

To the boy I fell in love with
But not in the right way

I was the sun and him storm clouds
Like night & day

Stunning together
But not everlasting

Sharing the skies
Violently parted by evening

He wanted all the action
Poetry, song and verse

I on the other hand
Wanted something more perverse

Fairytales by starlight
Shutter clicks at dawn

Innocent excursions
Romance; I hadn't planned on

Companionship opening to the world
Emotions not easily understood

Know my darling gentleman
I loved you as best I could

35
My Swan Song

Shelby Catalano

No death torments more
As the tune of true love lost
Woven harp strings taut
Takes its toll and pays the cost

Plucking fingers bloody
As the sounds become muddy

He left me staccatoing words
I thought about many things
Did he just give up on me, I thought?
As I loosened all the strings

Was there no choice left?
Has this song been reduced to theft?

The asexuality plucking, a crescendo

Hurtling notes, cutting cords
Strings popped; untethered
As he whispered haunted words

He begged me for sex
And just like that, the matter put to rest

Rejection plays its final refrain
My heartstrings, yet he wants brass
Snapping all my plans in half
A love never meant to truly last

I say goodbye, I end the song
Swan songs like this were never long

36

I Care For You, Dear Reader, Whomever You May be

Penelope Epple

I get it.
You're afraid. You're hurting.
You were lied to.
And you don't know how to deal with it.

I get it.
You were taught that
being alone is something to fear.
Without romance
why would you be worth anything to anyone?
Why should anyone care about you,
care for you,
if you cannot love them?
Why should you matter to anyone
if they cannot get your heart,
or your body, in return?

If they are going to care about you,
if they are going to love you,
don't you owe them that in return?

No.
You don't owe anyone your heart, your body.
Not even if they love you,
not even if they care about you.
You are not heartless or cruel for this.

You can love someone without your body.
You can care for someone without loving them.
You can be alone without being lonely.

I'm sorry you were lied to.
I'm sorry that you're scared.
I'm sorry you're in pain and want
to lash out so
someone else can hurt as you do.

We've been there too.
We know the intensity of what you feel.
We know.
I know.

I know.

Meet the
Co-Authors

Deborah Mejía

Deborah is an agender, panromantic-asexual Honduran writer that has been creating stories in her head in both Spanish and English since even before she could write. She values the importance of artistic storytelling to create mediums of empathy and human connection, and strives to bridge differences of race, identities, and beliefs through poetry, short fiction, and visual arts shared through her social media to create a world of curiosity, understanding, and equality accessible for everyone.

Amy Sutton

Amy is an acclaimed playwright and poet - their play 'A Human Write' has won awards in the Southern Counties Drama Festival and Scottish Community Drama Association, and their poem 'Love in Brighton' won second place in the Smeuse Poetry Competition. They live by the sea with their partner and a pair of very territorial chickens.

Niamh Donnelly

Niamh has been writing ever since her fingers could hold a pencil. She started writing poetry because of a boy, of course, but found love for all things poetic! Niamh is finishing her final year at school before carrying on to an English with Creative Writing course at University. She aspires to be a New York Times Best-Seller and won't stop until she's made it.

D. L. Cordero

D.L. Cordero is a published sci-fi fantasy author, performer, poet, and horror dabbler working out of Denver, CO. When not writing, they can be found wrangling their blind pit bull, obsessing over their ever-expanding garden, and breaking through binaries in every

way they can. You can read their work on dlcordero.com and follow them on Instagram, Twitter, and Facebook @dlcorderowrites.

Penelope Epple

Penelope Epple (Pronouns: [in writing] *e/h*/h*s, [in speech] they/them, e/em, one/ones) is a Queer AroAce Neutrois poet originally from Ft. Wayne, IN who is in the process of moving back to Cincinnati. *E has previously had h*s work published in The Aze Journal, X Marks the Spot, For a Better World 2019 and 2020, and Lions-on-Line. *E is currently working on some books of poetry with themes of queerness, Catholicism, exclusion and erasure, aroace love, and space.

Celeste Skywalk

Celeste is a 17-year-old high school student who has an instinct for writing. Writing followed her after she developed the art of passive reading and through games like crosswords, she found her way home: towards writing. On a sunny day, she might also swipe up and style dark academic outfits. She has a keen interest in Greek mythology that you can see on her social media handles. She paints a world through her quill. She is a music lover at heart too. You can follow her at @eurydicelived on Instagram, Twitter and Tumblr for long aesthetic poems and music-related posts. Her heart is filled with love and she believes in spreading the same, no matter what! Doesn't the world need more rainbows and unicorns to decorate the beautiful sky?

Niamh Hennessy

Niamh (she/they) is an Irish/Australian deim-aromantic asexual poet. They have been navigating their identity for decades and poetry has been a fundamental tool in that journey. Working as an engineering and yoga teacher, they believe that people are multifaceted and cannot be placed within one box and that life is about exploring all aspects of oneself. They reignited their love of writing, following the completion of university studies, as without deadlines writing could be a pleasure rather than a chore. You can find more of Niamh's creative expressions on their website balanceinchaos.me or on Instagram @balancein.chaos.

Vernajh Pinder

Vernajh Pinder is no stranger to poetry. He has been writing it since he was 10-years old. He uses poetry and reading as tools to help him escape reality, and it was through this, he fell in love with them. He released his first book titled 'Hope You Don't Get

Famous: Poetry and Prose' in October 2019. Vernajh holds a BS in Hospitality and Tourism Management from the University of Maryland Eastern Shore, where he provided the student commentary for their Spring 2019 Commencement Exercise. He is currently pursuing a Master's of Education with a specialization in School Counselling. Mr Pinder is a

Certified Hospitality Graduate, Certified Restaurant Server, and is ServSafe Certified. He received a plethora of scholastic awards and has been inducted into several honours societies.

Aamir Hassan

Aamir is a proud and out Queer person of colour living in the UK. He is an educator, podcast host and writer. He also delivers on LGBTQ+ Education and education around inclusivity and equality. Along with his husband, he is breaking down boundaries of what it means to be South Asian, Queer and out!

Lily Rosengard

Lily Rosengard (she/they) is an intersectional feminist activist and anti-racism advocate. Lily is a Londoner of Chinese, Canadian, Scottish, Jewish, English heritage, and much of Lily's writing is focused on liminality and their own lived experiences of queerness, mixed-raced identity, and mental health. Lily works in advocacy for a international NGO working for gender equality and girls rights. Lily loves cats, climbing, craftivism and bright colours. Lily holds an MA in Human Rights from UCL, and an undergraduate degree in Philosophy and Religious Studies from the University of Cambridge.

Catherine Guy

Catherine Guy is an author, artist, poet and performer, but first and foremost, she is human. A human who uses her art to start conversations, pour honey on wounds and wake the sleeping. Guy published her first book, 'The Wallflower That Bloomed', in March 2018 and her second book, 'Black Love Isn't A Myth' in 2020. Transcending boundaries, her books include works addressing a myriad of social issues including feminism, discrimination, racism, broken relationships, heartbreak, sexuality and abuse. At a young age, she learned that her voice was her power and so it became the weapon she never put down.

Taisha Guy

Taisha "That GUY" is a writer! Well, Human first. Guy writes socially aware pieces of poetry that shock the senses. Her approaches to topics about love and the social landscape are both thought-provoking and organic. It is vegan. Writing since the age of 13, Guy experienced her first heartbreak when a friend and ally on the American middle school battleground, moved away. She has never been without pen and paper since.

Adam Gaffen

Adam Gaffen is the author of the science fiction series The Cassidy Chronicles, which follow the adventures and experiences of Aiyana and Kendra Cassidy as they struggle to pull the human race into a new era of interstellar exploration. He lives in Colorado with his wife, five dogs, five cats, and is working on the fifth book in the series as well as a biography of Aiyana.

Paul Williams

An LGBTQ, Black-Hispanic young adult with an eclectic taste in music, Paul Williams has struggled with his identity, eventually leading to mental illness. However, with support from his siblings, he gained new confidence to express his inner emotions through art and writing.

Ankur Mondal

Ankur had Bachelors in Arts with comprehensive experience of 14 years in Advertising film making. He often walks out with his camera, to a random destination; exploring humanity and exploring life. His partner loves to discover and explore new destinations, and they tend to capture every precious moment they share. His greatest passions in life are Singing, Traveling and Photography. Through his photography and

writing, he seeks to document his personal experiences, capture scenes and events as he sees them and share the beauty and diversity of the world he has seen with others. Through his work, he wishes to portray the beauty, diversity, and hardship of the interlocking world. Singing helps him connect to his soul and also find him his Nirvana.

Melanie Williams

Melanie Williams is a queer poet and author who grew up as an emancipated minor in rural Australia. Williams writes subjective poetry about violence, sexuality, grief, abuse, love and identity.

Mollie Sambrook

Mollie is a 22-year-old internet poet and writer. Born in the southeast of England she is currently living in Manchester after completing an MA in Creative Writing. She is working on a second collection of poetry and is in the process of drafting a fantasy novel. After recently opening up about Bisexuality,

Mollie hopes to write stories that comfort those with shared experiences and challenge the minds of those who don't.

Christy Pineau

Christy Pineau (who goes by the pen-name C.P Harding) is a Freelance Content Writer who lives in Eastern Canada. She rediscovered her passion for the written word at the beginning of the pandemic and hopes to one day publish her autobiography. She currently runs a beauty blog that aids transgender women with beauty content and hopes to one day migrate to YouTube.

Ashley Amber

Ashley Amber is an emerging author and poet from Boston, Massachusetts. Ashley wrote her first picture book at the age of 9 when she entered a Reading Rainbow contest, earning a certificate from LeVar Burton. She's most recently known for her  debut novelette 'The Flip Side of Sad', as well as her personal poems on asexuality. When Ashley's not writing, she's making videos on Youtube as an "Authortuber" while she seeks a home in publishing for her LGBTQ+ book series.

Shelby Catalano

Shelby Catalano is an author of poetry and blog content, including her upcoming debut poetry collection 'From Hope to Heartbreak'. When not writing, she's found doing aerial arts or lurking in bookstores. She writes commonly around how romance  and emotion shape our perceptions – and the many imperceptible, yet haunting ways it carries with you. You can follow her on Twitter @sherubicat and visit www.shelbycatalano.com for news and future releases.

Tejaswi Subramanian

 Tejaswi is a journalist and public health researcher who believes that community care models are the way ahead to ensure a rights-based, feminist approach to people's health & well-being. They identify as Neuroqueer and hope to live in a world where their personhood is not seen as a quirk or oddity. Tejaswi enjoys spending time with their cat, cooking for loved ones, making tactile art, and at electronic rave dances.

Abhiti Gupta

Abhiti (She/Her) is a geek from
Delhi who still has to come out of
her closeted safe place. She reads
books to relive lost and lived
experiences of caste, gender,
sexuality, mental health and can be
found wandering with multiple
thoughts crossing her mind at
once. She works with a feminist public health organisation
and aspires to continue learning aspects of intersectional
feminism. She wants to do as much as possible in this life
through self-nurturing as a process. To be able to survive this
one life is her primary goal.

INKFEATHERS PUBLISHING

India's Most Author Friendly Publishing House

Stay updated about latest books, anthologies, events, exclusive offers, contests, product giveaways and other things that we do to support authors.

 Inkfeathers Publishing

 @InkfeathersPublishing

 @_Inkfeathers

 @Inkfeathers

 Inkfeathers.com

We'd love to connect with you!